A Knight's Bad Day

For Simon

This is a work of fiction. All characters, stories, legends, myths, places, and events in this novel are used fictitiously.

Taeran Arts, Pleasanton, CA 94566 USA

A KNIGHT'S BAD DAY

ISBN 978-0-9833236-5-5

TAERAN
ARTS

Long ago, a traveling knight came across a distant castle.

The knight, whose name was Egbert, needed a job.

In those days, a knight had to challenge all the other warriors to earn his spot in the king's hall.

In contests against each of the king's warriors, even the strongest, Egbert was victorious.

When the men went hunting the next day, Egbert saved the king from a vicious aurochs.

That night, in the hall . . . It was the custom in those days for warriors to brag about their accomplishments after dinner.

One warrior claimed: "As a lad new to battle, I killed thirty of the enemy and tamed a winged serpent that I rode across the sea and back in an afternoon. If I ever leave my lord on the field before the foe is vanquished, I will clean the floor of the hall with my tongue and give my armor to a scullery maid."

The warrior who told this story was hiding behind a tree when the aurochs attacked the king.

Another said, "I chased a half-human monster into a swamp. By the time I caught him, my rusted sword had split in two, and I killed the beast by biting on its neck."

And so they talked. After each warrior spoke, the king thanked the man for his fealty and rewarded him with gold, more to some than to others.

Then it was the new knight's turn to speak. You could almost hear the men groan, as they thought about how he would boast.

Egbert Tells his Story, Even Though No One Wants to Hear it.

When I was a young lad I sought the hall of a famous chieftain who lives across the sea.

I fought beside this chief until I became skilled at combat. The chief rewarded me well, but when none of my enemies and no man at his court could out-fight me, I left to test my strength. I traveled through many countries engaging challengers, and no one defeated me.

One day I came to a crossroads where a sightless old crone sat pulling stones from a bag.

She said, "What do you seek?"

"I seek to know if I can conquer the world."

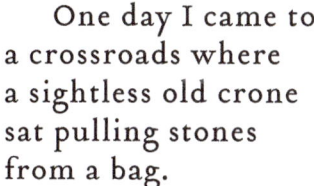

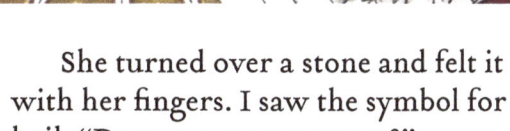

She turned over a stone and felt it with her fingers. I saw the symbol for hail. "Do you expect a storm?"

"No," she said. "The bad weather I see is for you alone. Can you be dissuaded from your quest?"

"No. I've weathered storms before."

"Have you? If you must, follow the yellow road until you come to a garden that is only visible by the light of the full moon."

I rode along the yellow road as fast as my horse could carry me. No full moon was due for a week, but within an hour I saw one rise in the sky.

I traveled until I saw two lads
patrolling a garden. The boys
were shooting arrows at the
retreating moon.
 "That will teach her to come
on the wrong night," said one.
 As far as I could tell they didn't
even notice me.

I passed them, dismounted,

and walked into a garden that
was unlike any I had ever seen.

Plants with leaves big
enough to hide
a man

sprouted
giant
flowers.

In the distance
rose an opulent palace.

When I knocked at the door, it was opened by a beautiful maiden. Inside were nineteen more.

The maidens led me to a hall where I was seated next to a Big Man with no hair. I could tell he was no warrior, but he was friendly and talkative. He giggled a lot, and I soon felt that I had known him all my life. I ate and drank as well or better than in any king's palace. He said, "You are welcome to stay as long as you like."

I was having such a good time that I forgot why I had come until the Big Man asked. "What brought you to my palace?"

I was forced to remember my quest. "I want to conquer the world."

"Oh, that's too bad," said the Big Man.

"Why is that?

"I know what you could do. But no, better not to."

"But I want to."

I pressed him for a while, and finally the Big Man relented. "You must awaken just before dawn and follow the path until you come to a man dressed in black with one arm, one leg, and one eye in the middle of his forehead.

"This man will direct you to a deep well. You must dive into it.

"On the bottom is a stone as heavy as three men that you must carry up to the surface.

"Once you get the stone onto dry earth, you must cleave it in half with one blow from your sword."

That didn't sound too difficult—or at least, not impossible. I knew that objects weighed less in water.

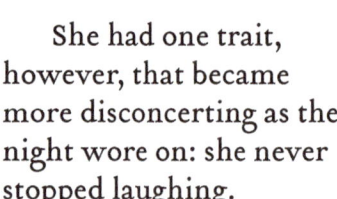

Then my host sent me off to my chamber with one of the beautiful maidens. "This is the custom among our people," he said, "and you must not insult the girl by refusing her."

She was very beautiful, as they all were, and I wouldn't have insulted her for a king's ransom.

She had one trait, however, that became more disconcerting as the night wore on: she never stopped laughing.

At dawn, the girl, still laughing, kissed me and reminded me of my quest.

I poured several pitchers of cold water over my head, put on my armor, and left.

After three days I ran out of food. On the fifth, I was chased in the wrong direction by a pack of aurochs, and on the sixth attacked by a boar.

As I traveled, the terrain became rougher, the hills craggier.

The trees whistled and moaned as if some torment had become too much to bear. Wild beasts growled in the distance and sometimes sounded as close as my shoulder. My horse balked.

Finally, after a week, I spotted the one-legged man dressed in black peering at me with his one eye. He flagged me down with his one arm.

What are you looking for?

Holy Grail?

Golden Fleece?

Goose?

Shoe that fits your one true love?

that lays the Golden Eggs?

Sleeping Princess?

He said, "I heard you were coming. Let's see . . . you're after the goose."

"Goose?"

"You know, goose, egg, gold, all that."

"Never heard of it, I'm—"

"Wait a minute, hold on, hold on. The grail, am I right?"

"No. Nothing to do with birds. I want—"

"I said grail, as in Holy Grail, not quail, you wally!"

"Well, I don't want any grail either, holy or otherwise. What I'm looking for is—"

"Stop. Don't tell me. It's the fleece."

"Wrong again."

"Sleeping princess? You kiss her, get the kingdom?"

"No."

"I've got it! You want the shoe that only fits your true love!"

"How about you let me tell you?"

"Oh, all right then. I give up. What do you want?"

"The location of a well."

"Oh that. Ha! Good. Serves you right."

"Go on," I said.

"One furlong straight ahead, left at the pollards, left, 16 paces straight, cross a meadow in the direction of the swollen foot oak, left, left again at the red leaf beech, right at the bramble, quick left when you see an apple and a maple growing together, climb a bank, go through a wood, come to a stream, follow it, you'll find the well. Got it?"

"Yes."

"Oh."

He sounded disappointed.

I followed his directions. The well I found wasn't the kind that men dig into the earth, but more like a puddle.

I waded in and looked for the stone the Big Man had described. What I found was nowhere near the weight of three men. This quest had turned into a waste of time.

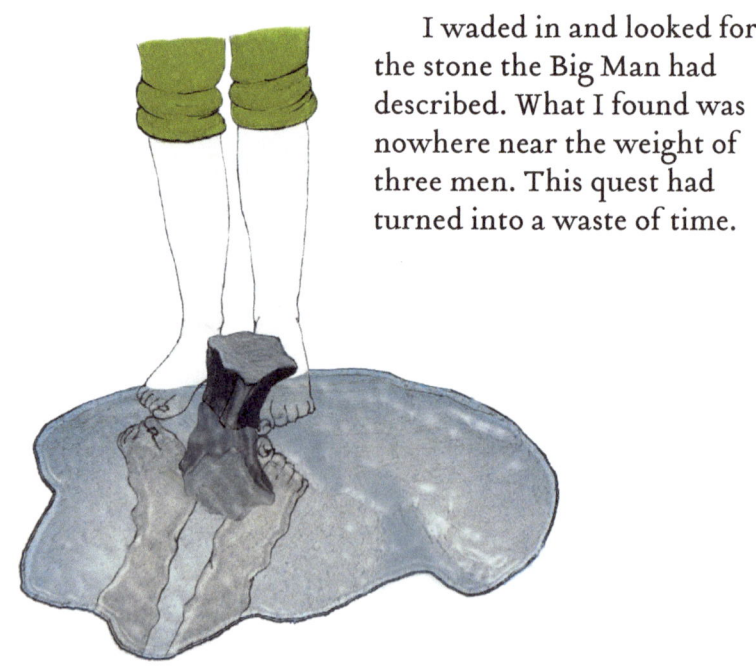

Having gone this far, I decided to see it through. I pulled out the stone, set it on the ground, and prepared to hack it in two with my sword.

All I expected to get for my trouble was a dull sword. But—

When my sword hit the rock, the sky turned as black as a moonless night. The wind roared. The earth heaved like a boat tossed at sea.

off balance   and tossed into the sky.   Then, when I came down . . .

I was thrown

The rain swirled, and hail the size of birds' eggs pelted down.

I ran to my horse

and protected

both our heads

with my shield.

After a while, the wind, rain, and hail stopped.
The sun shone as brightly as before.
The trees lay this way and that,
uprooted and thrown down by the storm.

The sky turned black again. There was no sound for a while until a voice bellowed so loud that the earth shook.

Who Challenges

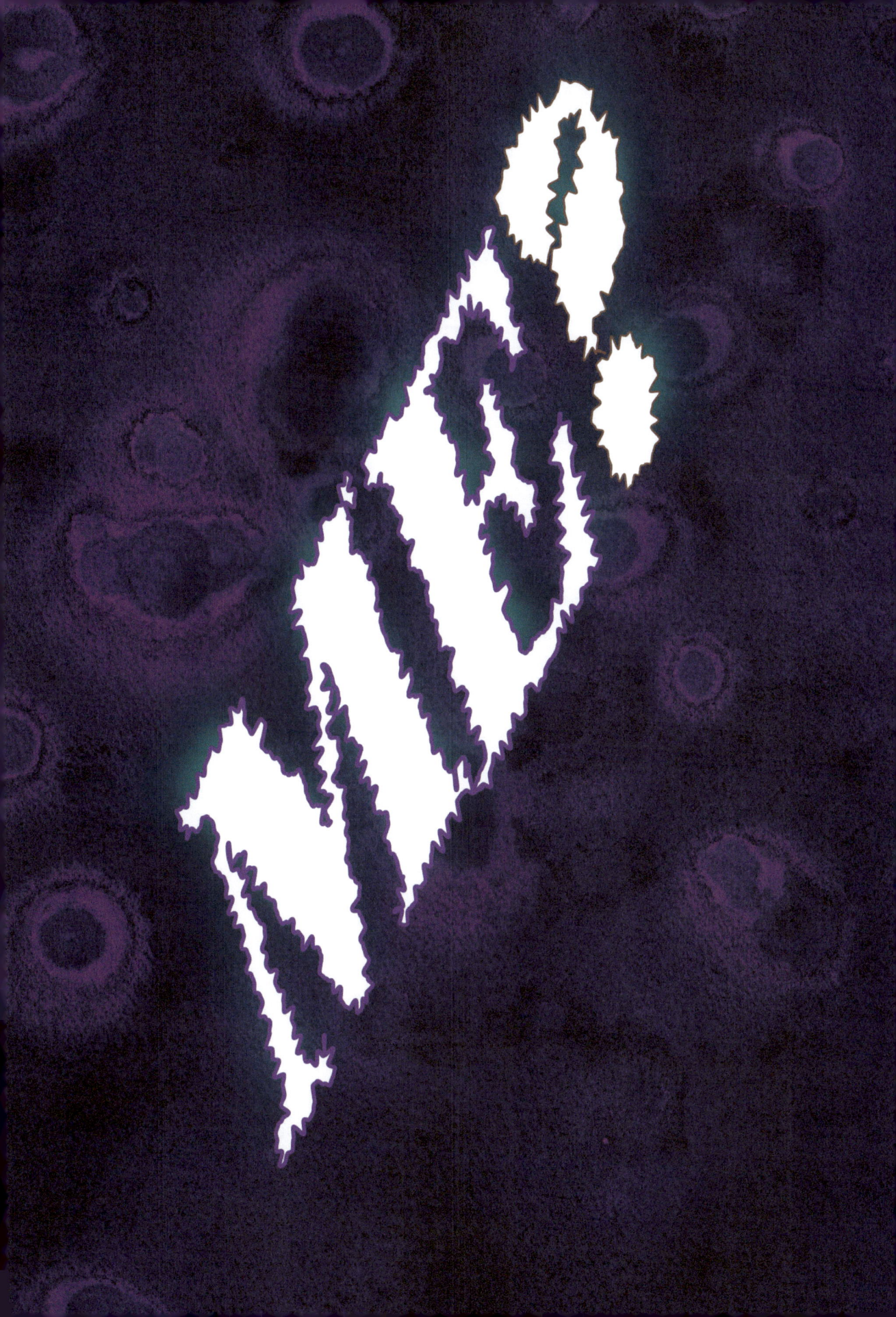

I scrambled out from under my horse. "I do," I said, a little softer than I meant to. I faced the creature, sword and shield at the ready.

It made a sound even more terrible than its bellowing. A blow from its sword exploded my shield.

I saw the creature ready to charge again and clasped my sword in both hands to fend it off.

When its sword hit mine, the sparks made new stars.

The beast struck my sword with such force that it flew from my hand. My weapon sailed toward my horse, and the terrified animal bolted.

I reached for my axe. Before it left my hand, the creature threw its axe at me. My skull was cut to the bone.

Now I had no shield, no sword, no axe, and no horse.

When I wiped the blood out of my eyes, my enemy was gone. He hadn't bothered to kill me or take my weapons. I crawled back to the golden palace.

I collapsed at the door of the enchanted hall. Twenty beautiful maidens bandaged me and put me in a room to rest where they left me, I thanked God, without any company.

In time I was well enough to attend a dinner with my hosts. Neither they, nor anyone else at the palace, ever asked me about my adventure.

Egbert sat down. His story was finished.

There was a stunned silence in the room for a moment or two when Egbert had finished his story. No one had ever heard a man tell a tale more to his discredit.

The there was a funny sound as one of the warriors tried to stifle a laugh. Everyone looked at him in horror, thinking that Egbert would dispatch him with a wine goblet.

But Egbert threw back his head and began to roar with laughter himself.

And before long every warrior in the room was laughing and telling the man next to him his own story about a time a fight had not gone exactly to plan.

The king gave a signal to one of his grooms who went to the door of the hall and led in a beautiful white horse. The king gave it to Egbert and thanked him for joining his court.

The men seemed to feel that Egbert wasn't so bad after all.
So, while he lost one battle, it seems he might have won another.

Other Books by Elaine Drew

ElaineDrew.com

www.ingramcontent.com/pod-product-compliance
Lightning Source LLC
Chambersburg PA
CBHW041537240626
47164CB00002B/45